Charles Francis Adams

An Oration

delivered before the municipal authorities of the city of Fall River, July 4,

1860 - Vol. 1

Charles Francis Adams

An Oration
*delivered before the municipal authorities of the city of Fall River, July 4, 1860 - Vol.
1*

ISBN/EAN: 9783337377663

Printed in Europe, USA, Canada, Australia, Japan

Cover: Foto ©Andreas Hilbeck / pixelio.de

More available books at **www.hansebooks.com**

O R

DE

MUNICIPA

OF THE

BY CHA

Fall River:

ALMY & MILNE, DAILY NEWS STEAM PRINTING HOUSE.
1860.

ORATION.

FELLOW CITIZENS:—After the lapse of eighty-four years, in which, at each recurring anniversary of this day, the brightest minds and the noblest hearts the land could boast, have strained their energies to elucidate the nature of the event we celebrate, as well as to honor the motives of those who became guides to our national success, I feel that I may be fully excused if I begin by presuming you sufficiently informed in regard to these matters. I shall not, therefore, attempt any detail of the history of the period, neither shall I enlarge upon the principles or the purposes set forth in the immortal State paper, the words of which are so familiar to every American ear. The past will take care of itself. What we have to do is with the present hour. The noble patriots of former days have gone to their reward. What we must consider is our own duty. No nation will prosper on recollections alone. Look at Greece and Rome, which have not fattened on the memory of thousands of years. The hour when men turn from the scenes around, only to fix their eyes on the dim distance behind them, when they strive, at the expense of their contemporaries, to magnify and exalt the heroism of their predecessors, dates the beginning of their effeminacy. The pages of Rome's greatest historian were not written until their author was a slave. There are persons among ourselves who actually believe that all virtue has departed, and that we have nought left but to sing pæans to the mighty dead. Whilst they delight to expatiate on the heroism that was, they as studiously avert their faces from the consideration of what heroism is. Yet nothing is more clear than the fact that the great battle of freedom did not terminate with the year 1776. It rages now to-day, and will rage to-morrow, and every day so long as we live. And all the value of the devotion which we pay to the manes of the departed will be better tested by the firmness and the energy with which we carry on our own share of the continuing conflict, than by the zeal with which we pile mountain high the flowers of rhetoric upon their graves.

This is no moment for lamentation or despair at our own shortcomings. Admit, if you will, that much of the action of the past few years has done us, as a nation, no great honor ; admit that grave errors of principle have been sanctioned in high places ; admit that the popular sentiment has, at times, been dangerously perverted ; admit, in fine, that the cardinal doctrines of our political faith, taught us in the great charter which annually, on this day, receives our seeming homage, are met with frigid coldness by many who officiate even the nearest to the shrine of our temple of Liberty. Admit all this, I say, if you please, and does it yet furnish the least excuse for faltering in the only course that can lead to nobler things ? No. The lesson of the day is addressed to *us*, and not to our fathers. It is ours to remove the wrong and reinstate the right. The sacred fire still smoulders, however much our high priests may have attempted to drown it with water. It is for us to revive the spark and to blow it once more into flame. And just in the proportion that our earnest efforts, under the favor of Divine Providence, meet with success in surmounting the obstacles that still beset the path of freedom ; obstacles, be it observed, but little less formidable than those that engaged the energies of our fathers ; just in that degree shall we be entitled to claim that modern degeneracy has not reached us. So may we boast of laying the cap-stone of a monument more enduring than any of brass or marble to the memory of the signers of the fourth of July.

Fellow citizens : I know not whether you have been made

aware of the fact, which I believe to be undeniable, that the Declaration of Independence is no longer received with unqualified favor in all parts of the United States alike. The reason is that it enunciates certain propositions touching human liberty as maxims beyond contradiction, the truth of which it is no longer convenient in some quarters to acknowledge. Hence has sprung up a reluctance to consider it without appending material modifications of its natural and obvious meaning. It is not long since some of its leading ideas were sneered at, as glittering generalities, by one himself not devoid of a most brilliant fancy, whilst on almost every day of the year, new and strange theories of construction are advanced, intended to deprive them of their vital force. All this, doubtless, you must understand, has its origin in some powerful cause ; for it is not the natural tendency of men to grow less in love with freedom, or of parties to relax in the support of popular doctrines. When, therefore, we see distinguished statesmen and orators, and learned lawyers, though still ready to heap empty laudation on the *men*, exercising their critical powers in nice refining about the *principles* of the Revolution, it is not unfair, I think, to presume some reason to be at the bottom of it, which it is advisable to bring to light. The outward visible sign is *reaction ;* and, strangely enough, it appears most extensively in those forms of political association which once were identified with the most extreme notions, not of American liberty, but of revolutionary France. Here it is that we find people preferring to dwell more on the dangers than on the blessings of Liberty. Yes, and even more than that. Here it is that the novel constructions to which I have alluded find the most acceptance. Constructions which I hesitate not to pronounce utterly at variance with the authority of the historical record, and with the declarations of the chief actors in the contest for Independence, as well as fatal to the perpetuity of really liberal institutions in every quarter of the globe.

With some of these heresies I propose on this day to do battle with what power I may. And I engage not the less strenuously because they are put forth by persons speaking with authority.

Conscious of the strength of my cause, I feel that with such armor, even a dwarf may successfuly cope with the sons of Anak.

1. And first of the first—What, fellow citizens, was the moving cause of the Revolutionary conflict? You will probably answer, as I do, that it was a question of Liberty. The Sovereign of Great Britain was trying to make slaves of our fathers, and they determined to be freemen. Hence the struggle and the victory. And hence it is that we are here to-day celebrating the declaration of our Independence.

Not so fast, my friends. This is all a mistake. We are now told in a high quarter that it was a question of *property*. That this is the primal cause of all the great struggles of the world; and that everything else is incidental. Listen to the words of one speaking with authority. " The right of property is sacred. And the *first* object of all human government is to make it secure. Life is always unsafe where property is not fully protected. To secure private proverty was a principal object of Magna Charta. Our own Revolution was provoked by that slight invasion upon the right of property, which consisted in the exaction of a trifling tax."

Such is the significant language of one learned in the law,* who, doubtless, had his reasons for magnifying what is after all, mainly the creation of law, the conventional understanding of men. Strange that Mr. Jefferson, in assigning the causes for the Revolution, in the Declaration of Independence, should have completely overlooked this one! Still more strange that we should always have thought that there were other and higher ones. What does the Declaration say?

" We hold these truths to be self-evident; that all men are created equal; that they are endowed by their Creator with certain inalienable rights; that among these are life, liberty, and the pursuit of happiness; that to secure these rights, governments are instituted among men, deriving their just powers from the consent of the governed; that whenever any form of government becomes destructive of these ends, it is the right of the

*The passage is taken from an article published last year, understood to be from the pen of the present Attorney General of the United States.

people to alter or abolish it, and to institute new governments," &c., &c.

Yes, you will observe that this paper says, " whenever any form of government becomes destructive of *these ends.*" What ends, pray ? Why the ends " for which governments are instituted among men.' And what are these ? They are, " the security of life, liberty, and the pursuit of happiness." Not a word here about property ! Not a word about " the *first* object of human government to make that secure." Not a word about the " slight invasion upon the right of property provoking the Revolution". · Mr. Jefferson forgot about this. *He* was thinking about something very different. What does he go on to say ?

" The history of the present king of Great Britain is a history of repeated injuries and usurpations, all having in direct object *the establishment of an absolute tyranny* over these States. To prove this, let facts be submitted to a candid world."

He then proceeds to enumerate eighteen different kinds of facts ; as, for example, he had refused his assent to wholesome laws ; he had called together legislative bodies at unsuitable places, for the purpose of fatiguing them into compliance with his measures ; he had refused to cause others to be elected ; he had endeavored to check the growth of these States ; he had obstructed the administration of justice ; he had made judges dependent on his will ; he had erected a multitude of new offices ; he had kept up standing armies in time of peace ; he had abdicated government by waging war against us ; he had plundered our seas, ravaged our coasts, &c. ; he had transported large armies of foreign mercenaries, to complete the work of tyranny ; he had constrained our fellow citizens, taken captive on the high seas, to bear arms against their country ; he had endeavored to incite the savages against us, &c., &c.

These are the offences which are stated to have provoked the Revolution. They are all offences against the lives, and the liberties, and the right to pursue happiness, of the people of the Colonies. They but remotely relate to their property. The only allusion to that subject is found, mixed in with many other grievances, in one of the articles, where it charges the sovereign with combining with others " for imposing taxes *without our consent.*" And even here, it will be observed, it is not the tax that is complained of, but the compulsion of the will which might otherwise be ready freely to grant it.

How different is all this from the pretence that the revolution was provoked by a slight invasion of the right of property ! It was *liberty* that was in question, and nothing else. It was the right of self control ; it was security of life from all capricious and tyrannical sway ; it was the right of man to pursue happiness in any innocent way, that stimulated the hearts of the people to resistance. It was this holy motive that sanctioned all the painful sacrifices which they endured, and hallowed every drop of blood which they shed as a votive offering to the future welfare of the human race.

And yet we have been told, by high legal authority, that security to life is but an incident to the *first* object of all human government, which is the security of property ! Of course it follows that security to liberty must fall still lower in the scale. It is not a good sign when the tendency of public men is to set up property—the most palpable of appeals to self-interest—above the higher sentiments of humanity. Who knows how far the best of us might yield to the temptation of making property of some of our neighbors, if we could only cover the pretension under the sacred shield of law ! But such a heresy finds no countenance in the great charter, the authority of which, even now, a large majority of this people still acknowledge. To us the moving cause of the Revolution yet remains ; and O ! may it ever continue so to appear, a question of human liberty, and nothing else.

But here a second proposition, of an equally startling character, though from a different quarter, presents itself to our consideration. Conceding the fact that the Declaration of Independence proclaimed a principle of Liberty, the question has been made, to whom of God's creatures it was intended to apply. Was it to all mankind, or only to a part ? If to all mankind, of course it must have embraced those who were at the time in a state of slavery ; and it is well known that there were more or less of this class to be found in every one of the Colonies. Was it contemplated by the framers of the instrument, that the new doctrine should, either directly or remotely, affect their condition ? To this question a negative answer has been lately given by a learned and distinguished jurist*, whose opinions on all subjects are entitled to the highest consideration. He maintains that when the fathers declared, in solemn tones, "*all* men to be created free and equal, and to be endowed with certain inalienable rights, among which are life, liberty, and the pursuit of happiness," they intended to describe only the governing,—that is, the white European race, of which they constituted a part. The question of liberty, therefore, was not raised in general maintenance of a principle for the benefit of mankind, but was a mere domestic difference among the whites, to settle the relation in which the one part which had gone to America should be regarded by the other part that had remained in Europe. According to him, then, nothing contained in the paper is to be construed as forbidding either portion of these whites from exercising any and every right of domination and control which they can obtain, by good means or bad, over the people of all other races known on the globe. In short, to use the very words of the authority I am quoting, our fathers " did not imagine that that instrument was to change the personal or political relations of their slaves."

Now I cannot stop at this place to point out to you the belittling nature of this new view of the action of our fathers. How mean they are made to appear in the boldness of their profession and the selfishness of their action. How false they stand, in boasting of resistance to tyranny in others, when they retain all the spirit of it within their own breasts. How dishonest they seem, in charging upon the king of Great Britain as offences justifying their refusal to obey his rightful authority, acts which in their nature bear no comparison as violations of human rights

---

*The Attorney General of the United States under the last Administration, in a speech made at New Haven, in Connecticut, in March last.

with those they were themselves determined to persevere in. I
must pass over all this, in order to go at once to the facts. Do
they bear out this remarkable construction of their motives ? If
they do, then we must abandon their defence, and claim for the
present generations in America, bad as they may be, the merit
of being, at least, better than their fathers.

The Declaration of Independence was made on the 4th of July
1776. The men who signed it all represented communities in
which persons were held as slaves. The question is, did they,
when making that declaration, suppose that it would have any
effect in changing their relations to those slaves.

And in answering this question, let me first of all consider the
position of the writer of the paper. He represented the Colony
of Virginia, largely holding slaves. What did Mr. Jefferson
mean should be done with them after Independence was declared ? Let his own account of himself answer the question.—
On the 2d of September, that is less than two months after the
Declaration, he resigned his seat in the Continental Congress in
order to take his place in the Legislature of his State, which he
did on the 7th of October. " I knew," these are his words,
" that our legislation, under the regal government, had many
very vicious points, which urgently required reformation, and I
thought I could be of more use in forwarding that work." And
so he changed his position, as he says in another place, " to
adapt our whole code to our republican form of government.—
Early, therefore, I moved and presented a bill for the revision of
the laws, which was passed on the 24th of October ; and on the
5th of November, Mr. Pendleton, Mr. Wythe, George Mason,
Thomas L. Lee and myself, were appointed a committee to exe-
cute the work."

This committee met, and apportioned the labor to the respective
members. Mr. Jefferson had his share, and in that share fell the
revision of the laws respecting slaves. Again I quote his own
words :

" The bill on the subject of slaves, was a mere digest of the existing laws
respecting them, without any intimation of a plan for a future and general

emancipation. It was thought better that this should be kept back, and attempted only *by way of amendment*, whenever the bill should be brought on. The principles of the amendment, however, were agreed on, that is to say, *the freedom of all born after a certain day*, and deportation at a proper age."

Now I ask whether Mr. Jefferson did not imagine that his own written testimony in the declaration did not pledge him to change the personal or political relations of the slaves. We see how earnestly and how immediately he applied himself to the work. It is very true, that in writing the account of it forty-five years afterwards, and explaining the reason why it was not done, he adds that " it was found the public mind would not yet bear the proposition, nor will it bear it even at this day." But he goes on to utter these most significant words : " Yet the day is not distant when it must bear and adopt it, or worse will follow.— *Nothing is more certainly written in the book of fate, than that these people are to be free.*"

Turning from this overwhelming testimony to the intent of the writer of the celebrated paper, let me now proceed to consider how its doctrine was applied in a wholly different section of the country. Out in the extreme north lived a community refusing to consider itself as within the jurisdiction of any of the thirteen States, and anxious to set up a separate government of its own, under which the people desired to be recognized as making an additional member of the confederacy. To this end, on the 2d day of July, 1777, just a year from the adoption of the resolution for independence, their delegates agreed upon a constitution and a bill of rights. The first article of that bill closely follows the Declaration itself, to wit :

"That all men are born eqally free and independent, and have certain natural, inherent and inalienable rights, among which are the enjoying and defending life and liberty ; acquiring, possessing, and protecting property, and pursuing and obtaining happiness and safety."

So far, the rule is in substance as taught on the 4th of July of the year before. But now comes the application.

" *Therefore,*" [I beg you to mark that word *therefore* ; it means 'for the reason above given,'] " no male person born in this country, or brought from over sea, ought to be holden by law to serve any person as a servant, slave or apprentice, after he arrives to the age of twenty-one years ; nor female, in like manner, after she arrives to the age of eighteen years, unless they are bound by their own consent, after they arrive to such age, &c., &c."

Now I respectfully ask, did not the people who drew this paper imagine that the Declaration was to change the personal or political relations of the slaves? They and their descendants established what is now known as the noble State of Vermont, and from that day of small things down to the present, in all the vicissitudes of their government, they have never ceased to be true to their primal pledge. They have construed the Declaration of 1776 not as a word but as a thing.

Of Massachusetts I trust I need not say much in this presence. You all know that her bill of rights prefixed to the Constitution of 1780, contains substantially the same article already quoted, excepting that it is not followed by a "*therefore*." But if the framers of the instrument did not themselves make the application, the Courts of the Commonwealth very soon supplied the deficiency. Slavery was never abolished here by law, because they decided that it could not exist in the face of these significant words in the Constitution. In New Hampshire and Connecticut the same consequences followed from direct legislation. Pennsylvania moved early, but did not complete her operation until a comparatively late period. "As to our law for the gradual abolition of slavery," said Timothy Matlack, a worthy and influential old citizen of that State, in 1817, " it was an expression of the will of the majority of the people, in support of the great first principle of our government, ' All men are born free and equal ;' and that majority has increased to a magnitude that promises unanimity." Rhode Island prohibited slavery by law in 1784, the year after the peace. New York followed suit in 1799, and New Jersey added her testimony to the rest in the year 1804. And yet we are told that our fathers did not imagine that that Declaration of 1776 was to change the personal or political relations of their slaves !

But, in order to complete this picture, it is necessary to go back once more to the action of Mr. Jefferson, and to show that his intentions were not limited to the sphere of the State of Vir-

ginia. So far from it, they were on the broadest scale of na-
tionality. So early as 1774, in the paper which he drew up as
a form of instructions to the first delegates from Virginia to the
Continental Congress,—a paper afterwards published under the
title of " A summary view of the rights of British America,"—
he expressly said that " the abolition of domestic slavery is the
great object of desire in those colonies where it was unhappily
introduced in their infant state,"—that is to say, all over the
country, from end to end. Now, to show that this was no mere
profession in him, let me remind you of what he did where he felt
he had the authority, even under the restricted powers of the
confederation. After the cession by Virginia of her western territory had closed up the great division among the States on the
subject of their rights to indefinite extension, and had vested the
title to these lands in the United States, Mr. Jefferson lost not a
moment in moving a committee in Congress, for the purpose of
organizing a form of government for the ceded country. This
committee was appointed, and consisted of Mr. Jefferson himself,
Mr. Chase of Maryland, and Mr. Howell of Rhode Island, all
three representing States where slavery yet existed, although in
Rhode Island it was then on the point of abolition. Yet this
committee soon afterwards reported a plan, based upon five propositions, the fifth and last of which was to this effect : that " after
the year 1800 of the Christian era, there shall be neither slavery
nor involuntary servitude in any of the said States, otherwise
than in punishment of crimes." For this provision sixteen out
of twenty-three members of the Congress present recorded their
votes. And even when counted by States, only three out of the
eleven present voted against it. It then failed only by reason of
a rule of order regulating the mode of putting the question ; and
it would have succeeded, even in spite of that, but for the ab-
sence of a single person who would have given effect to the affirm-
ative vote of New Jersey. But so decided was the sentiment on
this subject, that delay only had the effect of concentrating it
with more earnestness. A few months later, the same provision,
in an amended form, making the operation of the prohibition im-

mediate, instead of postponing it until 1800, was adopted by a unanimous vote, and thus did it happen that to the instigation of the author of the Declaration of Independence himself, the magnificent territory west of the Ohio owes its present ability to bow without hesitation to the force of the self-evident maxims which he had inserted in it with his own hand.

From this exposition I think I have succeeded in rescuing the fame of the fathers from the imputation that they were proclaiming a doctrine for others, upon which they never designed to practice themselves. So far from it, the fact seems to me undeniable that, down to a certain period, the effort to carry out the principle over the whole land by changing the relation of the slave, was energetic, constant and successful. After that time, it is true, and I am ready frankly to confess it, there came a marked difference in the public mind. The force of the Declaration seems to have in a degree exhausted itself. The acquisition of an immense additional territory adapted to slave labor, in conjunction with the invention of machinery facilitating the development of the culture of a new staple everywhere producible in the southern portion of it, raised up barriers to the farther progress of the old doctrine, which have proved more and more impassable with time. Instead of advance, we see multiplied the proofs of retrogression, until now, when the propositions once recognized as of universal application, are either cautiously limited or else flatly and totally denied. And we are gravely told, by a distinguished and discriminating slaveholder, that when our fathers advocated principles which they honestly believed would last forever, they had no idea of the extent to which the crop of cotton could be carried by slave labor in America, or they would forever have held their peace !*

Fellow citizens, this is not the first time that man has listened to the charm of the siren, and lost, in the grosser delights of sense, all consciousness of the high elevation to which it is his mission to aspire. What says the poet ?

*See the opening of the speech of Mr. Curry, of Alabama, in the House of Representatives, 14th March, 1860.

" The steep ascent must be with toil subdued ;
Watchings and cares must win the lofty prize
Proposed by Heaven : true bliss and real good."

The cotton that represents uncompensated labor, will never
bring money that can purchase undisturbed sleep to its possessor.
It is not for us, fallible creatures that we are, to condemn our
brethren for errors which, under similar temptations, we might
be equally liable to commit ourselves. But whilst we may make
suitable allowances for them, it would be inexcusable in us, in
our situation, to be deluded by their sophistry, or to be led to
copy their example. The difficulty now is that there are men
among us—yes, men of ability, learning and character, too,
which might adorn any station,—who are busily engaged in dis-
seminating these heresies as truth,—who are trying to make you
believe that the Declaration of Independence is a sham, and that
the world was made to breed slaves. This very heresy that I
have now been exposing to you, fundamentally subversive as it is
of every political principle which you have been taught from your
childhood, had its origin, indeed, in the slave producing regions,
but it now pervades the American atmosphere far beyond those
limits. It is repeated, commented upon, justified and expounded
boldly before crowds of listening freemen, with all the powers of
logic and all the arts of eloquence. It is settling into the convic-
tions of extensive associations. of people originally gathered for
the love of very opposite sentiments. It finds lodgment in the
trembling bosoms of the wealthy in our commercial cities, who,
in their study of the rise and fall of stocks, dread most of all to
be perplexed with fear of change. Wherever it may go, it carries with it poison to freedom. It emasculates the strongest citizen, by teaching him that force is God's highest law, to which,
when once established, his obedience in all cases is a duty. It
prepares him in very truth for the advent of that grim image,
armed to the teeth in steel and mounted on a fiery charger, already prefigured to us in the declamation of the orator upon
whose argument I have been commenting, before the thunders of
whose cannon all hearts shall quail, and what remains of the man-
liness of freedom shall be crushed from off the face of the land.

And this brings me to speak of a third doctrine, even more prevalent than the others, equally sustained by high authority, and yet in my belief not less destructive to the principles of the Declaration of Independence than either of its predecessors.

It is seriously maintained that the duty of the people of the United States is to take no note whatever of the growth and the spread of slavery, but to give free leave to every person or association of persons to establish it if they like, in any new spot within the jurisdiction of the United States that they may choose to select. In other words, if a new community shall think fit to apply in practice the doctrines of the Declaration, and make freedom the rule of society, so let it be. But if, on the other hand, it shall determine in favor of the law of force, subjecting one man and his progeny to labor for another man and his progeny without compensation to the end of time, then let that law prevail without interference and without complaint.

Now, if the principles of the Declaration be really self-evident truth, then is slavery a great evil, a flagrant violation of the rights of man, a gross outrage upon the fundamental maxims, for the establishment of which, in their own favor, our fathers fought and bled. The logical consequence necessarily is, that if we follow the recommendation not to intervene where we have the power to prevent it, if we suffer a community under our sanction, upon territory under our jurisdiction, to establish slavery, merely because it chooses to exact service without paying for it, then we, with our eyes open, consent to and approve of an act which we know and admit to be a flagrant violation of the rights of man, and a gross departure from the principles which our fathers, many of them, laid down their lives to establish.

Is this such a position as conscientious people ought to take ? Do they not, by permitting the commission of a great offence, under circumstances in which they could prevent it if they would, make the criminal act of others their own ?

Perhaps the force of this proposition may be better understood by a slight change in the mode of illustration. It is well known that in one of the territories belonging to the United States a form of society has been established in which, among many eccentric practices, the right of a man to a plurality of wives has been engrafted upon the religious code. This is not a novel institution in the history of the world. It dates back in antiquity quite as far as the practice of holding man in slavery, and is quite as well fortified by scripture example. Even at this day it is well settled law in a large portion of the Eastern world. Neither can it be pretended that as a pure question of morals it is open to any more condemnation, or that the bad consequences to society are any more serious than those entailed by the toleration of slavery. If then we are to permit the one without remonstrance in regions where we might prohibit it, why are we not just as much bound to sanction the other, provided the people like it? If the doctrine of non-intervention be sound in regard to slavery, why not likewise in regard to polygamy too?

But let me now carry you one step farther and relate what once happened in the territory of Judea. We are told by the historian that in the midst of that country there sprang up an association with a recognized chief and a social organization, one of whose customs was quite peculiar. They were called, in Latin, *Sicarii*, that is, stabbers; and their practice was to assassinate such of their neighbors as circumstances seemed to render fitting in their eyes at the moment. To that end they carried with them short daggers with which they inflicted a fatal wound so adroitly that not even the nearest bystander could detect the perpetrator of the deed. In this way they succeded in murdering even the high priest while sacrificing at the altar in the temple at Jerusalem. And the Jewish community, finding itself helpless to apply a remedy to this arbitrary practice, appealed to the authority of the Roman Governor to intervene and put a stop to it.

Now supposing that at Rome it had been announced by some high and leading senator that it would be dangerous to the peace of the nation to take any steps to prohibit this custom; that the true rule was to let every community do in respect to such mat

c

ters just what it might prefer. If they disliked the practice of private assassination enough to prohibit it, why let them do so. If, on the contrary, they thought it a wholesome institution, so let it be. In short, suppose this noble legislator had proclaimed that non-intervention was the great conservative key to all statesmanship. Let us once more imagine that we can transfer all this state of things from the province of Judea to a territory of the United States, and from the city of Rome to the city of Washington, and then I demand of you to answer me, how shall we stand released from our solemn responsibilities to the feeble settlers gathering under the shelter of the national protection, by the declaration that the attempt to intervene, to save them from danger, can only be done at the hazard of a greater danger to the Union, and therefore that nothing should be done at all. The pretence is as false to the country as the doctrine is treacherous to the rights of man. There can be no greater danger to the Union than the refusal to fulfil the duties which are incumbent alike upon all. There can be no greater shock to society than the denial of those benefits, the security of which constitutes its greatest value. If the obligation of the individual be obedience, that of the government is protection. In no social state conceivable can there be a release from this Siamese twin connection. It is not then possible to shift off the responsibility by a mere act of the will. It must co-exist with the relation, and it can terminate only by the annihilation of the conditions under which it was originally formed.

Let us not then seek to avoid the difficulties attending the full recognition of the terms of our first compact of Union, by the timid plea of non-intervention.. The mission of this people is to teach the value of well regulated liberty to the world. Let us not leave the solution of what remains unaccomplished of the experiment to chance, or caprice, or to malevolent opposition. We claim no right to interpose in the policy of existing States whether foreign or domestic. Let each manage its affairs in its own way. With the power to control, it must be presumed to possess the wisdom to correct whatever may be found amiss within its jurisdiction. But in all cases of inchoate organization, so long as the authority shall remain vested in the general government, intervention for the correction of present or for the prevention of future social evils is not only a right but a solemn duty. Without it we may be but nursing the scorpion that will ultimately destroy ourselves. We may be only sowing the seed of dragon's teeth to raise a crop of warriors armed for the subjection of the world.

Let me now occupy a moment in recapitulating the three heresies to Liberty, which it has been my aim to combat on this particular anniversary. They are

First, the assumption that the right of property is the *first* object of all human government, and that our revolution was provoked by a slight invasion of it.

This belittles all that was manly and heroic in the struggle by making it centre in a miserable selfishness.

Secondly, the pretence that a declaration of principles, purporting to be of the most universal application, was really intended by our fathers of 1776 for the benefit only of themselves of the white race, when in danger of the same kind of forcible subjection from abroad, which they reserved to exercise forever afterwards over their weaker brethren at home.

This at once impeaches the good faith of the patriots, and dishonors us their progeny for attempting to pass them off before the world as honest men.

Thirdly, the abnegation of the right of intervention to prevent the establishment of dangerous or vicious institutions within the jurisdiction of a government.

This undermines all sense of responsibility in statesmen for the consequences of their inaction in difficult conjunctures ; and puts at hazard the security of life, liberty and happiness, for which governments were instituted among men.

Fellow citizens, mark here what I say to you in truth and soberness. All these three heresies spring from one and the same source. They are the offspring of fear to meet the slave question in the face. It is this which perverts the feelings, which chills the hearts, and which obfuscates the intellects of some of the most exalted of the land. It is this which raises the mighty current of reaction, that threatens to back the stream of Liberty from its natural and genial flow over the entire surface of the republic.

Do you ask me what I would have you do in this emergency ? I trust I do not underestimate the magnitude of the power that

is bearing so hard upon the vital springs of freedom in America,
when I say, that by energy, by perseverance, and above all by
union among yourselves in the support of established truth, you
may yet resist it all.   To use the words of an old English poet,

> " We claim no power, when heresies grow bold,
> To coin new faith, but STILL DECLARE THE OLD."

The object to be attained is the revival to its fullest strength of
that sentiment imbibed from the Declaration of '76, which began
to fail so early as 1808, and which has exercised little real influence in the direction of public affairs ever since.   To this end the
celebrations of this Anniversary may be useful, provided they be
suitably improved.   But if gotten up merely to chant a hollow
lip-service to the image of past perfections, without the heart to
meet any present emergency, they are worse than worthless.—
For their tendency is only to deceive, by the appearance of devotion to a duty that is never done.   Trust me, the principles of
human Liberty are not safe until you inscribe them in letters of
living light on the portals of your Capital city—until you inspire
your government with a love not simply of abstractions on parch-
ment, but of realities in the seats of influence and power—until
you animate your political warriors to blow a trumpet that carries
no uncertain sound.   It is the characteristic of the nineteenth
century, above that of any of its predecessors, that governments
are directed by opinion.   They bow to the sentiment of the people.   Now what sort of a sign is it in America, when the seat of
your national government makes no cordial response to your most
approved doctrines of liberty ? when the men whom you put on
the highest pedestals of office turn their backs to the true deity*
you have been ever taught to reverence, and worship a gloomy
idol, the relic of a barbarous mythology ?   Whose fault is it that
these things are so ?   Whose fault is it that the leaders are timid
and halting and equivocating and treacherous in their service ?
Is it theirs ?   I answer, No, not altogether.   They are not afraid
of their adversaries.   They are afraid of *you*.   They tremble lest
enough of you should desert, or grow lukewarm, or listen to false
and designing teachers, to bring on their defeat.   If you can be
depended upon to be firm, persevering, inflexible and *united*, there
will be no need of farther care for the issue.   The victory is already won ; and the banner of freedom will soon again float proud-
ly over the battlements of the State, once more the emblem of an
honest and a consistent people R B   9, 3.

* At the right hand of the speaker stood a beautiful young girl with the dress and in-
signia appropriate to the goddess of Liberty, whilst arranged on each side were thirty-
three more representing the respective States of the Union.

www.ingramcontent.com/pod-product-compliance
Lightning Source LLC
Chambersburg PA
CBHW020626260626
47157CB00009B/3195